## *Someone* Was in Big Trouble!

Suddenly the door to the cafeteria flew open. Mrs. Kieffer came striding through. She looked around the room. Then she began purposefully walking toward our side of it. Everyone turned to stare at her. She had a look on her face like she meant business. As she got closer, she looked as if she were heading directly to our table.

I glared at Reed. Now she would get what she deserved. She would get in trouble in front of the entire fifth and sixth grades.

Mrs. Kieffer finally stopped at the head of our table, and stood there staring down at all of us. *Here it comes, Reed Litwin,* I thought to myself.

But it turned out not to be Reed after all.

"Jeanine Hoffman, please come to Mr. Gray's office at once," Mrs. Kieffer demanded.

Suddenly everybody was staring at me. Even though I knew I hadn't stolen Mrs. Kieffer's gradebook, I *felt* like a thief. . . .

# THE LOCKER THIEF

Shannon Gilligan

A BANTAM SKYLARK BOOK®

New York • Toronto • London • Sydney • Auckland

RL 4, 008–012

THE LOCKER THIEF
A Bantam Skylark Book / June 1991

Skylark Books is a registered trademark of Bantam Books, a division of
Bantam Doubleday Dell Publishing Group, Inc. Registered in U.S. Patent
and Trademark Office and elsewhere.

ISBN 0-553-15895-3

Published simultaneously in the United States and Canada

---

Bantam Books are published by Bantam Books, a division of Bantam Doubleday Dell
Publishing Group, Inc. Its trademark, consisting of the words "Bantam Books" and
the portrayal of a rooster, is Registered in U.S. Patent and Trademark Office and in
other countries. Marca Registrada. Bantam Books, 666 Fifth Avenue, New York, New
York 10103.

---

PRINTED IN THE UNITED STATES OF AMERICA

CWO        0 9 8 7 6 5 4 3 2 1

# Contents

# 1

........................................

# Gang Meeting

**I** knocked on the back door of Davey Johnston's house.

His grandmother, Matta, answered it. "Hi, Jeanine," she said. "Come on in."

"Thanks," I said as I stepped inside. The kitchen smelled of fresh brownies.

"Everyone else is waiting for you upstairs. Can you take a plate of these up with you?" Matta asked with a wink.

"You bet," I answered. I picked up a plate of brownies and headed up the back stairs to the third floor.

The third floor of Davey's house is really the attic, and the new winter headquarters of Our Secret Gang. Before the weather got cold, we used to meet outside in the chicken coop in Davey's yard.

# Shannon Gilligan

The members of Our Secret Gang are Jason Fox, Nancy Mitchell, Davey Johnston, and me—Jeanine Hoffman.

"Hi, everybody," I called, nudging the door open with my foot because I was holding the plate of brownies in both hands. "Sorry I'm late. Basketball practice ran late."

"Hi, Jeanine," Nancy said.

"I'll take those." Jason hopped up. Even though Jason is only in fifth grade, and Davey and I are in sixth grade, he's the tallest of all four of us.

"I know *you'll* take them," I said, laughing. Jason eats like a horse.

"You're not late at all," Davey told me. "I was just calling the meeting to order."

Davey is president of Our Secret Gang. He runs our meetings, although when he isn't around, I do it. I'm vice president of the gang.

I took off my jacket and scarf.

"Why did practice go late?" Nancy asked.

"We had to nominate people for team captain," I answered.

"Did you get nominated?" Nancy sounded hopeful.

"Yup." I took a bite of one of Matta's warm brownies.

"Jeanine, that's great," Jason said between chews.

"Congratulations," Davey added.

"Well, I haven't been elected yet," I reminded them.

"Who else was nominated?" Nancy asked.

"A whole bunch of people at first. Then they kept having runoffs until only two of us were left," I told them. "It's down to me and Linda Loomis."

"Linda Loomis?" Nancy cried. "But she's so quiet. I didn't even know she played basketball."

Nancy is by far the shiest member of Our Secret Gang, so it gives you an idea of just how quiet Linda Loomis is.

"She may seem really quiet, but she's a demon on the court. She's really, really competitive," I replied.

"Silent but deadly, huh?" Jason said. I looked at Nancy and smiled.

"Okay, I officially call this meeting of the Millerton chapter of Our Secret Gang to order," Davey said. "The first item on our agenda is a report from the treasurer. Jason?"

"Right. Let's see," Jason said, suddenly getting serious. Jason loves money just about as much as he loves food. He opened his treasurer's notebook and started to read. Meanwhile, Nancy, who is gang secretary, started to record minutes of the meeting in her notebook.

"We had sixty-two dollars and thirty-seven cents in our passbook savings account last month," Jason announced. "We made twenty-six cents in interest this month. With this week's member dues of four dollars, the grand total comes to sixty-six dollars and sixty-three cents. We'll owe my mother ten dollars for the answering service for the month. So that brings us back to fifty-six dollars and sixty-three cents. Any questions?" Jason finished.

"Not here," Davey answered.

"Me, neither," Nancy added.

The reason we pay Jason's mother for an answering service is that Our Secret Gang also operates a detective agency. We didn't start out solving mysteries. At first, we met so that we could talk to each other about our secrets. The whole thing had been Davey's idea. In order to become a member of the gang, you had to reveal your deepest secret to the other members. And you had to keep everyone else's secret a secret, too. Even our name was a secret.

But shortly after school started this past September, things changed. The four of us solved the mystery of the missing hands on the museum clock. It was a big deal because the clock hands turned out to be stolen and made of solid gold. We got our picture in the paper, and each of us received a hundred-dollar savings bond from Mr. Dolan, the town mayor. After that, we decided to start a detective business. We couldn't use our club's real name, Our Secret Gang, because we were sworn to secrecy. So we decided to call ourselves the Millerton Detective Gang instead. That's how Jason's mom answers our line: "Hello. Millerton Detective Gang. Can I help you?" It sounds really professional.

"Speaking of the answering service, have we gotten any calls lately?" I asked.

Jason started to chuckle. Nancy smiled.

"Mrs. Maxwell called again this morning," Davey said. "She wants two of us to come by later."

I groaned. "Her glasses again?"

Davey nodded. Mrs. Maxwell is as blind as a bat, and about once a week now she calls us to come find her glasses. Without them, she can barely find her way around the house. They're usually in some obvious place where she can't see them, like on the bookshelf next to the television set. But once we found them in the refrigerator.

"At least we make some money," Jason commented. "Three dollars each time."

"I'm not complaining," I said. "It's just that I wish we'd get another mystery. A real one this time."

"One is bound to come up soon," Davey pointed out. "So far we've gotten a big case approximately every five-point-two weeks. We're due for one any day."

Davey is a math genius. He's usually pretty careful to hide it around other people, because he doesn't want people to find out. But around us, he can be himself.

"I wonder if there are fewer crimes in the winter when it gets cold and snows," I said.

"Let's hope not," Jason replied.

"It's my turn to go to Mrs. Maxwell's today," Nancy said cheerfully. "I like her."

"I'll go with you while Matta drives Jason and Jeanine home," Davey offered. "Any other business?"

"Before we go, I want to make sure this meeting schedule is going to work out for everyone," I said.

We had changed our meeting schedule because now I have basketball practice every day after school. We used to meet on Mondays and Thursdays. Last week we had changed to Tuesdays after practice and Saturday mornings.

"Fine here," Jason said. "The only problem might be Saturdays when I visit my dad. But I think I can get him to give me rides."

Jason's parents had just separated, and he was still getting used to seeing his dad on just the weekends. "We can always change the time or something, if things don't work out," Davey volunteered.

"I don't have any problem with the schedule," Nancy said. "It works fine for me."

Just as Davey was about to close the meeting, I remembered something else.

"Before I forget, I can't meet with anybody at lunch tomorrow. There's a new kid starting in my homeroom, and I'm her First-Day Buddy," I announced.

"You are?" Nancy asked. "I wish you'd been my First-Day Buddy."

"I know." I smiled at Nancy. "Me, too."

First-Day Buddy is this program that was created over the summer by our principal, Mr. Gray. He'd learned about it at some camp for teachers. First-Day Buddies take new people around to all their new classes; explain about the lockers, buses, and clubs; and introduce new students to other kids and the teachers. In other words, if you're picked, you're the new kid's buddy for the first day, and according to Mr. Gray, it really helps kids adjust.

Nancy was a new kid at MLK, that's short for Martin Luther King Elementary, last January, before the First-Day Buddy program started.

"Look on the bright side, Nancy," Jason said. "First-Day Buddy is supposed to be someone in your homeroom. You could have gotten *me* for First-Day Buddy. Then think what shape you'd be in."

Nancy groaned. "You're right."

"Do you know anything about the new girl yet?" Davey asked.

"Just that she's from Los Angeles," I replied.

"If there's anything I can do to help you, just let me know," Nancy offered.

"Thanks, Nancy," I said.

"Okay. So everyone will meet here again at ten o'clock Saturday morning?" Davey asked.

"Unless your math is right and we have a new mystery before then," Nancy said.

"Let's cross our fingers," I said.

"Good. Then I move we close the meeting" Davey announced.

"I second the motion," Jason added.

"See everybody tomorrow in school," Davey said.

Nancy snapped her notebook shut. We stood up, got our coats and things together, and trooped down the back stairs to meet Matta.

"When will the basketball team be voting for captain?" Jason asked as we headed down the stairs.

"Not until next week," I answered. "Everyone gets to watch how we play in the meantime. Linda and I have to take turns leading off the drills. We even have to make a speech about why we would make a good captain."

"Boy, Coach Kimball doesn't fool around," Jason remarked.

"No, but that's why the team is so good," I replied. "We were second in the district last year. This year, we're trying to be first."

When we got outside, we all said good-bye. Jason and I got in the car with Matta, and Nancy and Davey headed off to Mrs. Maxwell's. I couldn't wait to find out where her glasses were this time.

# 2

## The New Girl

**M**atta dropped Jason off at his house first. Then she headed toward mine.

"How's everything at home?" she asked.

I don't like talking about my home situation too much, even with Matta. She doesn't know my secret, but sometimes I think she understands.

"Everything's fine," I answered. "My parents are in Palm Beach on vacation," I added a second later.

"Will they be coming home for Christmas?" she asked.

"I think so," I said, trying to sound cheerful. The truth was, I probably wouldn't know until the last minute.

"How's Ella?" Matta asked as we pulled into our driveway.

"Great." This time, I didn't feel like I had to hide anything. Ella Fairfax is our housekeeper, and she really is great.

"Well, send her my very best," Matta said as I climbed out of the car.

"I will," I promised. "Thanks for the ride."

I live in a big house on the outskirts of Millerton with my family. This basically consists of me; my sixteen-year-old sister, Lisette; Ella; and Joseph West, our caretaker. I don't count my parents as part of my family because they're never home. That's my secret, the one I told Davey when we first started the gang. My parents don't even know I'm alive.

This sounds like an exaggeration, but it's true. My dad is president of the family business, the Hoffman Corporation. He travels on business about seventy percent of the time, and my mom always goes with him. When they're not working, they're off someplace like St. Bart's with all their rich friends. This time, they were on vacation in Palm Beach, Florida, and I wasn't even sure if they'd come home for Christmas.

A lot of kids in Millerton think I don't have any problems because my family is so rich. Our house is really big, and I have my own horse. But they have no idea how bad it can be when you're totally ignored. I kept track of how many days my parents were home last year, and it was only forty-seven. Davey said that was only three-point-nine days per month.

And I bet no other parents forgot their kid's birthday this year. Luckily, Our Secret Gang had planned a surprise party for me that day after school. It was a perfect example of why I love being part of the gang. I'd felt terrible, and then the gang made me feel a whole lot better. My friends can't make my parents spend any more time at home, or notice me when they are here. But they make me feel like I belong someplace. It makes a real difference.

Since I don't get along very well with my sister, the person I love most in the world is Ella. Sometimes I pretend that she's my real mother.

"I'm back here!" Ella called after I yelled hello. I headed toward the kitchen, expecting to find her cooking dinner. Instead, the kitchen was empty.

"Ella?" I called.

"I'm in my living room," she said.

Ella has a few rooms off the kitchen. There's a bedroom, a bathroom, and a small living room. She was lying stretched out on her couch.

"I was just getting up," she said, yawning.

Lately Ella's been tired a lot. I've been getting more and more worried about it.

"Did you make an appointment with Dr. Weber for a checkup?" I asked.

"I have one on Friday," Ella replied. "Don't you go worrying about me in the meantime. I'm just getting old. How was school?"

When she sat up, I noticed there were dark circles under her eyes.

"School was okay," I said.

"Okay? That's all? How was basketball practice?" Ella wanted to know.

"I got nominated for team captain. We vote next week."

"I'm not surprised," Ella said, grinning. She gave me a big hug, and we headed into the kitchen.

"Is there anything I can do to help for dinner?" I asked.

"Dinner is all ready, but can you set the table?" she said.

"Right away."

Ella started to fix a salad while I got out the dishes.

"I'm First-Day Buddy for a new girl in my homeroom tomorrow," I said. "She's from Los Angeles."

# OUR SECRET GANG

Before Ella could say anything, the back door slammed. Joseph never slams it, so I knew it was Lisette.

"Hi, Ella," she called.

"Hello, Miss Lisette," Ella said cheerfully. "How was your day?"

Ella calls Lisette "Miss Lisette" because she's the oldest daughter in the family. Ella says it's a habit from growing up in Tennessee. Lisette's name *used* to be Elizabeth, until she went to ballet camp in Paris two years ago. When she came back, she had changed her name to Lisette. She says it's going to be her stage name when she becomes a professional ballerina.

"Practice was really hard," Lisette said as she came into the kitchen. "Harold had us do pirouettes for forty-five minutes."

Harold is Lisette's ballet teacher. She goes to ballet class for two hours every day after school, and four hours on Saturdays. She has ballet posters all over the walls in her bedroom, and a whole shelf full of ballet books. If you ask me, she's one big ballet bore.

"Oh, hi, Jeanine" she said finally, noticing me. She sat down at the table while I set it.

"What's your chore?" I asked, placing a fork on a napkin.

"Give me a break, Jeanine. I just got home!" Lisette snapped.

"Well, I just got home, too," I returned.

"Girls, please," Ella said.

Lisette stuck her tongue out at me and grabbed the mail. I made a face back and finished setting the table. She sat like that for a while, sifting through the letters and advertisements, until she remembered something.

"Oh, Jeanine," she said in her sweetest possible voice.

I immediately became suspicious. The only time Lisette is nice to me is when she wants something.

"Yes, your highness," I said.

"I was wondering if you'd heard about the new girl in sixth grade at MLK," she asked.

"She's going to be in my homeroom," I answered. "I can tell you a lot more about her tomorrow. I'm her First-Day Buddy."

"You *are*?" Lisette said.

"Yes. Why?"

Lisette shrugged. "Her dad's just a movie producer."

**16**

"How do you know?" I asked.

"Some girls were talking about him at ballet class," Lisette answered casually. She paused, pretending to be interested in a flier from a grocery store. "He produced *To Dream to Dance*."

So that was it! *To Dream to Dance* was a ballet film that was a big hit last Christmas. Lisette must have seen it five times.

"I get it. You want a part in his next film, right?" I said.

"Don't be silly." Lisette paused. "It's not so far-fetched, you know. Harold says I'm really good. Just find out if her father's doing any more dance films, okay?"

Lisette really bugs me. When she wants something from me, she's really nice. The rest of the time, she doesn't know I'm alive. When she got a car for her sixteenth birthday, she was supposed to drive me places. So far she's driven me to one gang meeting in three months.

"I'll find out as much as I can," I said, "on one condition."

"What?" Lisette said.

"I get ten rides, any time and any place I want."

Lisette hesitated, then said, "Okay."

Ella put a roast chicken with onions down on the table. "Dinner's ready," she announced, smiling at the two of us.

Lisette was really nice to me for the rest of the night. She asked if I wanted to watch a program on the Kirov Ballet with her and even said good night.

The next morning, I almost fell off my chair when she offered to drive me to school.

"I won't even count it as one of your ten rides," she promised.

On the way, she reminded me about what she wanted. "Find out everything you can from the new girl. Maybe you could have her over this weekend."

"I'll see if I like her first," I said.

"Well, try to like her, okay?" Lisette replied as she dropped me off at the curb in front of MLK.

I headed straight for the school secretary's office, where I was supposed to pick up the new student.

"Hi, Mrs. Wentworth. I'm here for . . ." I began. My words trailed off when I spotted the girl on the bench. She was wearing a black leather motorcycle jacket, a black miniskirt, and green lace tights under black suede boots that came up above her knees. Not only that, she was wearing sunglasses.

"Hi. I'm Reed," she said, standing up. She held out her hand to shake mine. "Reed Litwin." Then she pulled her glasses up on her forehead as if she were at the beach. "Are you my First-Day Buddy?"

"Uh . . . yeah," I replied. "I'm Jeanine Hoffman."

"Reed is going to be in your homeroom, Jeanine," Mrs. Wentworth told me. "She has her schedule already. It's very similar to yours."

I nodded. "Mrs. Kieffer explained that to me yesterday."

Mrs. Kieffer, my homeroom teacher, had told me what to do and what to expect. But I don't think there's really any way to prepare a First-Day Buddy for someone who looked like Reed. I turned to take another look. Her outfit was unbelievable. It made her look more like a senior in high school than a sixth-grader.

"We'd better get going," I suggested.

"I know. I've got a ton of questions," Reed said.

I thanked Mrs. Wentworth and took Reed out into the hall. "Do you know who I am?" Reed asked as soon as we started walking toward the fifth- and sixth-grade wing.

"Well, sort of," I replied.

"I'm the daughter of Samuel Litwin, the famous film producer," she announced.

"My sister told me," I said.

"In Los Angeles, I'm really popular, especially with boys," Reed continued. "Which brings me to my next question."

I waited to hear what she said next.

"Who's the cutest guy in our class, and who's going out with him? Because I've got news for her. She's got some new competition." She let out a huge laugh.

A bunch of people turned to stare. Practically everybody we passed was already staring at Reed's outfit. Even Wanda Evarts, who has a whole collection of fish earrings in different neon colors, couldn't take her eyes off Reed.

Although Davey's one of my best friends, I thought he was the cutest guy in our class. But I wasn't about to tell Reed about him.

Instead, I started to explain that we had two lunch periods at MLK, because the cafeteria was too small to fit everyone at once. I also told her that attendance was taken every morning in homeroom;

that we had French and art three times a week; and that you had to sign out in the teacher's log if you wanted to go to the bathroom.

Reed didn't hear a thing I said. She kept scouting the hallway for boys, and when she saw one she liked, she would interrupt me and ask his name. She didn't seem to pay attention until I started talking about lockers.

"So there are no locks on our lockers?" Reed asked again, as if she couldn't believe it. "Don't things get stolen?"

"Locks are against school rules, and so is stealing," I explained. "They really stress honesty at MLK and in Millerton."

"And I suppose you're going to tell me that it works, right?" Reed said. She gave me a superior smile as if I were in about second grade.

"Listen, I'm sure there's lots of crime in Los Angeles, but it's different here. This is the country," I told her. "Every once in a while something is taken. After all, there are about a hundred fifth- and sixth-graders using these halls. But it hardly ever happens."

Reed whirled toward me, her eyes flashing with anger. "Let's get one thing straight, Jeanine. I'm the one from Los Angeles, so don't tell me about crime there. You've probably lived in this hick town all your life."

"Millerton is not a hick town," I said hotly.

"Oh yeah?" Reed retorted. "Then where are the malls and the art museums? What about bookstores and gourmet food takeouts?"

I was about to reply that at least we didn't choke to death on smog. But then the bell rang.

"Come on. We've got to go to homeroom," I said.

"I can't believe I'm stuck with you all day," Reed muttered.

"Neither can I," I grumbled.

During homeroom, which lasts fifteen minutes, I decided to try really hard to be nicer to Reed. I wished I hadn't lost my temper, even if she had acted like a jerk.

But things only got worse. For the rest of the morning, Reed kept making comments about all her famous friends in Los Angeles and how much better things were out there. She said she had seen a few cute guys at MLK, but that they were nothing compared with the boys at her old school. She thought all the teachers were boring, and she didn't want to hear about any activities or clubs. According to her, basketball was a dumb sport. The only thing she was even half interested in was cheerleading. When she heard that cheerleading didn't start until junior high, next year, she said, "We'll see about that." By lunch, I was going nuts. I could have killed her.

Luckily, Eleanor Randall, who wants to be an actress, had been hovering around us all morning. She asked to sit with us in the cafeteria, so while Reed was bragging about how huge her closet was back in her old house in Los Angeles, I was able to escape for a few minutes at least to look for Nancy.

"Hey, where's the new girl?" Nancy asked, when I found her on the opposite side of the cafeteria.

"Eating with Eleanor," I replied.

"I heard she's got a famous dad. What's she like?" Nancy asked.

"Impossible," I answered, rolling my eyes. "All she talks about is boys and how much better everything is in Los Angeles. Her next favorite subjects are the movie business and clothes. She asked me if MLK had a fashion designers club."

"A fashion designers club?" Nancy echoed.

"*Yes*. She was president of the one at her old school," I explained.

"Well, then she's with the right people now," Nancy said, looking in Reed's direction.

Besides Eleanor, Reed was sitting with Bonnie Turner and Cynthia Malinowski. They both love clothes. They look as if they loved Reed, too. They were hanging on her every word.

"Just pray I get through the day," I said. "I may be the only First-Day Buddy ever to choke a new student."

Nancy giggled. "It sounds as if she deserves it. Hey, did Davey tell you where we found Mrs. Maxwell's glasses?"

I shook my head.

"In the bread box," Nancy told me.

I couldn't believe it. Mrs. Maxwell was too much.

I sat with Nancy until the bell rang for fifth period.

"Back to the lion's den," I announced.

"Good luck," Nancy said sympathetically.

The afternoon didn't turn out to be as awful as I expected. Eleanor ended up taking Reed around most of the time. I hung in the background.

Reed turned out to speak perfect French, and Madame Roux, our French teacher, got all hyped up. When she found out Reed had spent all her summers in France, she made her give the class a talk about daily French life. I wanted to throw up when she said, "Reed, you can be my teacher's helper for this class. You're much more advanced than the rest of the students."

Reed smiled, then threw a snotty glance in my direction. I just looked the other way.

The day was finally over. Before we split up to go to our lockers, I asked Reed if she had any questions about school procedures.

"No," she replied, before turning on her heel and marching off. "I can figure this school out by myself," she called over her shoulder.

While I was dumping my books in my locker, Eleanor Randall ran up. "Isn't Reed neat? She has the coolest clothes!"

I didn't want to say anything, so I just shrugged. But that wasn't enough for Eleanor.

"I'm so excited to have her in our class," she said. "Aren't you?"

"It should be interesting," was all I could manage to say.

# 3

# Locker Thief!

For the next few days, I didn't see much of Reed. I ignored her in class, and whenever I passed her in the halls, she was deep in conversation with Melinda Dalton, Suzy Fredette, and Eleanor, the three biggest snobs in our class. A few times, Reed stopped talking when I went by. I was sure she wanted to let me know that they were discussing me, but I was too busy with basketball practice, schoolwork, and the gang to care.

I didn't talk to Reed again until the following Monday. In the middle of basketball practice, I broke a shoelace and ran back into the girls' locker room to get a new one. Reed was standing in front of the locker room bulletin board, hanging something up.

"You scared me," she said, whirling around. "What are you doing here?"

"Getting a shoelace. What are you doing here?" I asked in return.

"Hanging up a sign," she replied defensively. "Is that against the rules?"

"No." I brushed past her and got my shoelace out of my locker. When I started back toward the gym, Reed was gone. We were in the middle of some drills, so I didn't have time to read the sign Reed had put up. All I noticed were the words "Cheerleading Tryouts" in big swirly letters.

Back in the locker room after practice, someone suddenly cried out, "My bracelet is missing!"

I turned to see who had said it. It was Linda Loomis.

"Are you sure?" Evie Woods asked.

"I'm positive," Linda said. She was pretty upset. "It was right here, in the pocket of my jeans. I always put it there during practice."

A bunch of kids clustered around.

"Was it that really nice silver bracelet with the turquoise?" Jolene Nichols asked.

Linda nodded.

"Go through all your stuff," Ellen Hayes barked from the far end of the bench.

## OUR SECRET GANG

While Linda went through her locker again, several girls started crawling around on the floor and looking under the benches.

"It's gross under here," Jenny Roper cried. She held up a blackened hand.

"Yuck," Meryl Macmullen said. "It's probably never been cleaned."

Linda turned the pockets of her jeans inside out and then slumped down on the bench. "It's not here."

"Tell Coach Kimball," someone said.

"Put a sign up on the bulletin board," I suggested. "Maybe someone else will find it."

We looked around for a few more minutes, but the bracelet didn't show up. Then someone ran in and announced that the bus was waiting.

"Get the driver to wait a minute," I said. In the meantime, we all hurried to finish changing and get our things.

"Sorry about your bracelet," I said to Linda on the ride home. "Is there a chance you didn't wear it today?"

"I'm almost positive I did, but I'll check," Linda answered. She looked out the window and didn't say anything more.

The next day at practice, Linda didn't mention

her missing bracelet, and I forgot to ask. I didn't think about it again until two days later, when Mrs. Kieffer made an announcement after lunch.

"Class," she began, "Esther Bariffi is missing her new red cardigan sweater. It was taken from her locker some time this morning."

Everybody started to whisper back and forth.

"If someone has accidentally taken the sweater, could you please see that it is returned to the front office by the end of the day today?" Mrs. Kieffer gave us all a stern look and added, "That's all."

As the class filed out of the room, Davey came up alongside me.

"Boy, we haven't had a theft at school in a while," he said.

"That may not be true," I replied. "The other day, Linda Loomis was missing a bracelet after basketball practice. She said she'd left it in the pocket of her jeans, which were in her locker."

"Did she find it?" Davey asked.

"I don't know. I'll ask her at practice today," I answered. I thought about Reed's being in the locker room in the middle of practice the same day that the bracelet disappeared, but I didn't tell Davey. I decided to wait until I talked to Linda.

When I saw Linda in the locker room before

practice, I asked her if her bracelet had turned up. She glanced around nervously at our teammates, who were getting dressed.

"No. I never found it," she said in a low voice. "And I got in a lot of trouble with my parents about it. The bracelet used to belong to my grandmother."

"Did you report it to Mrs. Wentworth?" I asked.

Linda nodded. "No one's turned it in."

That night after dinner, I called Davey.

"There's something I didn't mention earlier. I wanted to talk to Linda first," I explained. Then I told him about finding Reed hanging up the sign in the locker room during practice that day.

"It might just be a coincidence," Davey said. "I wouldn't say anything to anybody else yet. Let's see if Esther's sweater shows up before we decide there's a locker thief."

"Right," I agreed.

Friday morning, there still was no sign of Esther's sweater. Davey and I had agreed on the phone the night before that we would discuss it at lunch with Jason and Nancy. The two of them already knew about the sweater from their homeroom teacher, but I hadn't told them about Linda's bracelet.

I was sitting down in the cafeteria with Davey and Jason when Nancy hurried up.

"Davey, I think your math was right," she said breathlessly as she sat down next to me.

"What do you mean?" he asked.

"Remember how you said that we'd gotten a big case about every five-point-two weeks, and we were due for one any day? Well, Jonathan Turner just reported that twelve dollars was stolen out of his social studies book this morning," Nancy announced. "The book was in his locker. I heard Mr. Newport talking about it with Ms. Larsen."

"Twelve dollars?" Jason asked, his eyes wide.

Nancy nodded. "I think we have a new mystery on our hands."

"Did you learn anything else?" Davey asked.

"That makes three locker thefts in one week," Davey said.

"Three? I thought there were only two," Jason said.

I quickly explained about Linda's bracelet. I also told them about spotting Reed that day when she was hanging up the sign for a cheerleading squad.

"I'm not sure it's Reed, Jeanine," Nancy said. "I know you don't like her, but she seems pretty serious about this cheerleading stuff. I doubt she would go to all the trouble of hanging a sign just so she could steal Linda's bracelet during practice."

I agreed with Nancy, but I was still suspicious. Reed had acted startled when she saw me.

"There's definitely a locker thief in the school," Jason said, "and all the thefts have happened in the fifth- and sixth-grade wing."

"Which means that the thief is probably a fifth- or sixth-grader," added Nancy.

"Then we've got about a hundred possible suspects," I chimed in. *One in particular*, I added silently.

Davey looked deep in concentration. "The first thing to do is narrow down the suspects."

"How?" Nancy asked.

"It should be simple," Davey began, "but we'll need all five homeroom teachers' attendance lists for each day that something was stolen. We'll also need the bathroom logs for each of those days."

"That way, we can tell who was here what day and who was absent," I said. "I can get the attendance lists from Mrs. Wentworth. She really likes me. I'll tell her that I'm working on a case."

"And I'll copy down the bathroom logs for Mrs. Kieffer's room and Mrs. Bell's," Jason said.

"I can get Mr. Newport's bathroom logs," volunteered Nancy.

"That leaves Mr. McClure's bathroom log. I've got science this afternoon, so I can get that," Davey said.

"Anything else, Davey?" Jason asked.

"Yes. Let's interview Esther, Jon, and Linda tomorrow at our Saturday meeting," Davey said. "They might give us some clues."

"Great idea, Davey," Jason said, just as the bell for the next period began. "So, we'll meet at your house at ten."

*In the meantime, Reed Litwin,* I thought, *I'm going to watch you like a hawk.*

# 4

**Eliminating Suspects**

That afternoon at practice, Coach Kimball decided to concentrate on shooting drills. Our first game was only two weeks away. When my turn came, I caught a pass from the coach and dribbled the ball up to the basket. I took a shot, and the ball dropped through the net with a *thonk.*

"Good shot, Jeanine," Coach Kimball called.

I nodded and ran back to get into the line at midcourt. Linda Loomis was ahead of me.

"Linda, can you talk to the Millerton Detective Gang tomorrow morning at Davey's house?" I asked.

"Why do you want to talk with me?" she asked.

"We're investigating the locker thefts and think there might be a pattern," I said. "The gang wants to talk to everybody who's had something taken."

35

"What else has been stolen besides my bracelet and Esther's sweater?" Linda asked.

"Jonathan Turner is missing twelve dollars from his social studies book. It was in his locker before lunch this morning," I replied. "Didn't you hear everybody talking about it after lunch?"

She shook her head. "No. I'd like to help you out, Jeanine, but I have to go shopping with my mom tomorrow. Could you ask me some questions now?" she replied.

*The gang will be disappointed*, I thought, *but maybe I can learn something from her now.*

"Did anybody see you put the bracelet in your pocket that day before practice?" I asked.

Linda bit her lip. "I don't think so. But I didn't try to hide that I was doing it. I always put the bracelet in my pocket when I changed into shorts."

"Had you talked about the bracelet to anybody? Or had anyone asked you about it?" I asked.

"No. I've been wearing it all year," Linda replied. "No one has noticed it recently that I remember."

"Loomis, Hoffman, pay attention," Coach Kimball yelled. We were almost at the front of the line again.

"Sorry," I whispered to Linda. "I didn't mean to get you in trouble."

"Don't worry," she answered, then took off toward the basket.

I didn't get a chance to ask Linda any more questions. She disappeared right after practice. But I probably knew enough for our investigation. After all, I'd been right there when Linda had discovered the bracelet was missing.

Before leaving school, I remembered to ask Mrs. Wentworth for the attendance lists for Monday, Thursday, and Friday. I was worried she might not give them to me. But she didn't seem to mind after I'd explained the gang was looking into the thefts. She rustled around her desk for a minute, then handed me a couple of sheets. I thanked her and ran to catch the bus.

That night, Ella made Southern fried chicken and mashed potatoes, my favorite dinner. As usual, Lisette spent the evening grilling me about Reed and her father. She was convinced that I'd ruined her career by not becoming friends with Reed.

I was pretty sick of Reed Litwin, and when I finally told this to Lisette, she left me alone.

\* \* \*

The next morning at Davey's, I told everybody about my talk with Linda, and Nancy took notes. Jonathan arrived to be interviewed just as I was finishing.

Jonathan told us he'd put the money in his book before school. "I thought it would be safe in my locker."

"Did anyone know that you brought that much money to school with you?" Nancy asked.

"Only Ramsey Twichell. He and I were going to go to Forbidden Universe to buy comics after school," Jonathan explained. "We'd been saving up."

"When did you notice the money was missing?" Jason asked. "Before first lunch period," he answered. "That's when I went to get my book for social studies."

"Which means the money was taken sometime between first and third periods on Friday," Davey noted. "The book was still there, right?"

"Yes. Wait a minute," Jonathan said. He sounded excited. "No one else knew where the money was, but first thing Friday morning, Ramsey asked if I'd brought it. We were standing right near my locker when he asked."

"So anyone standing nearby could have heard that you brought money with you to buy comics?" I asked.

Jonathan nodded. "Boy, would I like to get my hands on the thief."

"One more question," said Davey. "What number is your locker?"

"Four-forty-one," Jonathan replied.

We thanked him for his help, asked him not to talk too much about our investigation to anyone—we wanted to keep a low profile—and told him we'd call as soon as we found out anything.

Our interview with Esther didn't help us find a suspect, either.

"A lot of people knew about my sweater," she told us. "I'd just gotten it. Sheila Dodge and Annie Osgood made a big fuss about it in homeroom the morning of the day it was stolen. And a lot of people complimented me on it in the halls Thursday morning before I took it off," Esther said.

"What period did you take it off?" I asked.

"Fourth period, right before lunch," Esther replied. "I had art, and I didn't want to get it all dirty."

"So anybody in the hall changing classes could have seen you put your sweater in your locker," Davey stated. "What number is your locker?"

Esther's locker was number 433.

"Do you think you can find my sweater?" she asked at the end of her interview.

"We don't have any suspects yet," Davey said.

Esther looked disappointed.

"Don't worry," I added quickly. "We haven't had an unsolved case yet."

"Thanks," she said as she was leaving. "I really appreciate what you guys are doing."

After Esther left, we turned to look at each other.

"At least we know when each of the thefts took place," Nancy commented.

"Right," Davey said. "The next thing we need to do is make a list of everybody in all three fifth-grade classes and the two sixth-grade classes. That's a total of ninety-nine kids. Then we can eliminate as suspects anybody who wasn't in school on any of those days."

"The attendance lists will do that for us. The people who weren't at school are marked by a little red dot," I replied.

"Why don't we combine all the absents on one big list?" Jason suggested. He was examining the three lists from Monday, Thursday, and Friday. "Who's Jorge Esposito?" he asked. "He's in my grade, and I've never even heard of him."

"That's because he's doesn't come most days," Nancy said.

"He was out all three days," Jason said.

"Well, we know Jorge didn't do it," I said, and we all laughed.

We spent the next half hour eliminating possible suspects. After we'd ruled out the people who had been absent, plus Esther, Linda, Jonathan, and the four of us, we had twenty-one fewer suspects.

"That still leaves seventy-eight fifth- and sixth-graders who might have done it," Nancy complained. "We'll never figure out who the locker thief is."

"We could narrow down the list even more if we could figure out if the thief is a girl or a boy," Jason pointed out. "Which do you think it is?"

"Well, there's been a girl's bracelet stolen from the girls' locker room, a girls' sweater, and twelve dollars," I stated. "If I were going to make a guess, I'd say that the thief is a girl."

"But that's still just a guess," Davey said. "We can't really be sure. Let's look at the bathroom sign-out logs to see who signed out Thursday during fourth period, *and* between first and third periods on Friday. We know those are the times when the stolen objects were taken."

## Shannon Gilligan

We knelt over the bathroom sign-out lists and began counting. Six people had signed out on Thursday during fourth period.

"Look. Reed Litwin is one of them," I said.

Then we checked Friday's list for periods one through three. A total of nineteen kids had signed out.

"Billy Gagliardi signed out during both those times," Davey observed.

We stared at the lists some more.

"Mary Ann Hockney is signed out both days," Jason said.

"So is Linda, but she isn't a suspect," Nancy added.

"Look," I said, pointing to Friday's list and trying to hide my excitement. "Reed again."

The other three gang members looked at me.

"And she was in the locker room during the middle of practice on Monday," Jason stated slowly.

"You may be right about her, Jeanine," Nancy said.

"I didn't like her from the moment I met her," I answered. "And it strikes me as awfully strange that stuff hadn't been stolen from the lockers in ages, and all of a sudden there were three thefts the week after she arrived."

42

"What about Mary Ann and Billy? Reed looks like a definite possibility, but so do they," Davey reminded me.

"Let's watch all three of them," Jason suggested.

"Good idea," Davey agreed.

"I can watch Reed. We have practically the same schedule. That's why I was her First-Day Buddy," I told them.

"I'll watch Billy," Davey said, "but he has as many fifth-grade classes as sixth-grade ones." Billy was actually supposed to be in seventh grade. He wasn't a very good student, and he was a bully besides.

"I'll keep an eye on him, too," Jason said.

"I've got Mary Ann in my homeroom and about three quarters of my classes," Nancy said. "I'll watch her, but I don't think she did it."

"Why?" we all asked.

"Well, look at the bathroom sign-out sheets. She goes to the bathroom about once every period. She must have a weak bladder."

"Keep an eye on her anyway," Jason said.

"We'll exchange information at the end of the day on Monday," Davey said.

*Reed Litwin, you'd better watch your step,* I thought.

# 5

. . . . . . . . . . . . . . . . . . . . . . . . . . . . .

# Bad News

I spent most of the following day with Sapphire, my horse. I brushed and groomed her coat, then took her out of the stable for a while. Since basketball practice had begun, I'd been too busy to spend a lot of time with her, and I'd missed her. I could tell she'd missed me, too.

Monday came. I could barely wait to start investigating again. I asked Lisette for one of my ten rides. I wanted to be at school early, before Reed got there, so I could watch her every move. When I arrived, there were only a few kids around. None of the buses had gotten there yet. I noticed that several teachers were standing at the ends of the hallways. I didn't think it was anything but a coincidence until Mrs. Kieffer made homeroom announcements twenty-five minutes later.

"There will be hall monitors posted at the end of each hall every morning and every afternoon until the thefts stop and the culprit is found. During class changes, we teachers will be patrolling the halls, as well," she announced. "Mr. Gray has also asked that students not leave anything of value in their lockers. This includes money, jewelry, or anything of personal value."

"So, what do we do with those things?" Earl Wetherby asked.

"Leave them at home. Or with your homeroom teacher," Mrs. Kieffer replied. "Homeroom is dismissed. You can go to your first-period classes now."

I looked over at Reed. She was looking for something in her backpack. Then she stood up. A few seconds later, I followed, making sure to hang back about three or four people so she wouldn't suspect anything. She went to her locker. Since it was at the other end of the hall from mine, I decided to get a drink at the water fountain. That way, I could keep a better lookout.

"Jeanine, other people might want a drink, you know." Ellen Hayes was right behind me.

"Oh, sure. Sorry," I said. I stood up, wiped my

mouth with the back of my hand, and pretended to adjust my backpack. Reed finally started to move, and I moved with her. She went straight to Ms. Larsen's for social studies. I followed right after her and watched her all class long, but she didn't sign out for the bathroom or act suspicious in any way. Science with Mr. McClure was next, but she didn't make any suspicious moves there, either. Finally, during art class, third period, she went up to Ms. Cook's desk and signed out on the bathroom sheet.

*Aha!* I thought. I rushed up to sign out, too.

"Jeanine, please don't run," Ms. Cook said. "Walk."

"Yes, Ms. Cook," I replied solemnly.

I got out into the hallway just as Reed disappeared around the corner. I followed her into the bathroom and got into the stall next to her. When she went to wash her hands, I decided to wait a few seconds before going out. Reed saw me come up to the sink next to her, but she didn't say anything. She just frowned. Then she went straight back to art class.

By lunch, I was beginning to get a little bored. Reed wasn't doing anything unusual, and it was kind of a pain to watch her so closely.

I sat with Davey at lunch. "Not much is happening with Reed," I told him.

"Whoever the crook is probably decided to take a couple of days off," Davey replied. "Everybody's on the lookout."

"You're right," I agreed. "Has Billy behaved strangely?"

"Billy *always* behaves strangely," Davey said.

After lunch, I stopped looking at Reed so much and started paying more attention in class. Thief or no thief, if I spent too many days like today, my grades would go down the tubes.

I wasn't sure what to do during practice. Reed could steal to her heart's content while I was there, and I couldn't do a thing about it. But it turned out that I didn't have to worry. Reed got on the early bus with Cynthia. I overheard them say they were going home to design swimsuits for next summer.

Basketball practice was really tough. Linda and I had to take turns leading the drills. I led the chest passes, then Linda did the bounce passes, and it was my turn to lead off again with more passing. After that, we did something called a rapid-fire drill. That's where one person stands in the center of a circle of people, and she has to go around the circle passing at each one nonstop until her arms are ready to fall off. I was glad Linda got to start that one! For the second half of the practice, Coach Kimball divided us into two teams for a scrimmage. Linda and I were on opposite sides. Coach Kimball probably wanted to see how we played against each other. Everybody on the team watched us closely. Voting for captain was only five days off.

I made three baskets pretty quickly. I was dribbling the ball up the court to make a fourth when Linda ran into me so hard, she knocked the wind out of me. Coach Kimball blew his whistle.

"Jeanine, are you okay?" he asked.

I couldn't talk. I could only nod.

"Linda, I know that was an accident, but a referee might not see it that way. Make sure to be careful," Coach Kimball said.

"Yes, sir," she mumbled, staring at the floor. "Sorry, Jeanine," Linda added. Her face was all red and sweaty.

"That's okay," I said when I could breathe again.

"Jeanine, you sit this one out," Coach said. He waved at Elizabeth Harrison. "Replace Jeanine." Then he blew the whistle.

I walked to the side of the court.

"Boy, Linda hit you hard," Jolene commented. I sat on the bench.

"I know," I said.

"You were playing really well," Jolene added.

"Thanks."

I was feeling stiff by the time I got off the bus at my house forty minutes later. I was going to ask Ella if I could borrow her special bath salts for aches and take a bath. When I got in the door, the phone was ringing. It rang two more times, so I answered it. *Ella must be out someplace*, I thought.

"Hello, this is Dr. Weber's office," said a woman on the other end of the line. "Is this Ella Fairfax's residence?"

"Yes, it is," I replied. "But I don't know where she is right now. May I take a message?"

"Yes, please do," the woman replied. "Please tell her that we've just gotten the results of some of her tests, and the doctor must speak to her as soon as possible. Do you think you can get this message to her this afternoon?"

"Yes, but why as soon as possible?" I asked. I had this sinking feeling in my stomach. "Is it serious?"

The woman paused. "I . . . er . . . can't really say. Please just have Mrs. Fairfax call the doctor as soon as possible."

"I will," I replied. For a minute, I couldn't move. I just stood there holding the phone. Ella was sick? I couldn't believe it.

"Hi there, sugar," Ella said, coming in with some packages. "Who was that? You look like you saw a ghost."

"That was the doctor's office, Ella. The woman said for you to call back right away. It has something to do with the tests," I answered woodenly.

I'd been so caught up in the locker thief at school, and basketball besides, that I had totally forgotten to even ask Ella how her doctor's appointment had gone on Friday.

A small look of fear crossed Ella's face. Then it disappeared.

"I'll call him right now," she said. Her voice sounded strange. "You go upstairs and take a shower."

"Can't I find out what the doctor says first?" I pleaded.

"Come down as soon as you're finished, and I'll tell you," Ella replied.

In the shower, I thought that maybe I had misjudged the situation. Maybe it wasn't serious at all. Maybe the doctor's assistant was just being professional.

I toweled myself dry and quickly put on some clothes. When I got downstairs to the kitchen, Ella was sitting at the table next to the phone. She was staring into space.

"What did they say?" I asked.

Ella looked up and smiled. "I have to go into the hospital on Wednesday. They want to do some more tests."

"What kind of tests? Why do you have to go into the hospital for them?"

"I don't understand exactly," Ella said. "They're going to stick a tube in a vein in my arm and snake it to my heart. That way, they can get a picture of my heart."

"Why do they want to look at your heart?" I asked.

"I guess they want to see if it's ticking right. I only know one thing for sure, honey. It's no use worrying over it until we see how the picture comes out." Ella stood up. "Now, how about helping me with dinner?"

# OUR SECRET GANG

As I stood there chopping green peppers for a salad, all I could think about was Ella's heart and how she might be really sick. But every time I tried to talk about it, Ella refused to discuss anything.

My one consolation was that Lisette was at a friend's for dinner. At least I wouldn't have to deal with her.

Right after dinner, Davey called. I told him about Ella.

"Gosh, Jeanine, I hope she's all right," he said.

I could tell he was thinking the same thing I was. If anything happened to Ella, I'd practically be an orphan.

"Are you going to call your parents?" he asked.

"Yup. As soon as I hang up," I replied. "How did everything go this afternoon?" I added, changing the subject.

"Nothing came up. Other than trying to poison the fish tank in the art room, Billy was completely unsuspicious," Davey reported.

"Did you stop him?" I asked.

"No, I didn't have to. Ms. Cook caught him and sent him to Mr. Gray's office," Davey replied.

"How about Mary Ann? Did Nancy see anything funny?" I asked.

"No, but she went to the bathroom so often, Mrs. Kieffer asked her if she was sick during spelling," Davey said. We both chuckled.

After we said good-bye, I dialed the number of the house where my parents were staying with friends in Palm Beach.

"I'm sorry, but Mr. and Mrs. Hoffman have gone out with the Ellises," a voice said. "Who did you say was calling?"

"It's Jeanine—their daughter, in case they've forgotten they have one," I snapped. "Could you tell them it's urgent?" Then I slammed down the receiver.

# 6

•••••••••••••••••••••••••••••••

# A Nasty Twist

The next morning, Lisette shook me awake.

"Jeanine, wake up," she whispered.

"What is it?" I asked.

"Ella. Last night after I got in, she told me about going to the hospital. I'm really worried," Lisette said.

"So am I," I replied.

"What would happen to us if Ella really were sick?" Lisette looked frightened.

I shrugged. "Let's hope she's okay."

"I'm going to call Mom and Dad," Lisette announced.

"I already did, last night," I told her. "They were out."

"I'll try them later. But listen. We have to be

really brave in the meantime," Lisette said, "for Ella's sake."

"I know," I said. "Who's going to take Ella to the hospital on Wednesday?"

"I am. I'm skipping ballet," Lisette said.

Lisette never skips ballet. I was beginning to wonder if she wasn't human after all.

"You should come, too," she said.

"Right. I can miss basketball," I said. Before the election for captain of the team, it was important to be at every practice. But election or no election, I wanted to be *with* Ella.

"Hey, where is everybody?" Ella yelled from the bottom of the stairs. "I made French toast!"

Lisette smiled at me. "Well, at least she hasn't lost her appetite."

That day at school, I tried to be extra careful about watching Reed. And I thought I was doing a pretty good job—until I followed her into the girls' room during math. She was standing in front of the mirror combing her hair. When I walked in, she shot me a mean look. "What *is* your problem?" she demanded.

"What's yours?" I retorted, heading toward a stall.

## OUR SECRET GANG

"Whenever I come to the bathroom, you follow me. You've been following me all day. Are you some kind of weirdo?" she asked.

"The only thing that's weird is your mind," I tossed back. "Only someone as strange as you, Reed Litwin, would blame somebody for a simple coincidence." With that, I slammed the door of the stall shut. My hands were shaking. I had almost blown my cover! If I wasn't careful, I might ruin our whole investigation.

For the rest of the morning, I tried to be less conspicuous. I even lost Reed at the beginning of lunch period. I was putting things in my locker. The next thing I knew, she was gone. She showed up in the cafeteria about fifteen minutes later with Eleanor.

"There she is," I said. But Davey didn't hear me. He was talking to Tim Kennedy, a new kid in Jason and Nancy's homeroom. They were discussing something about electronics.

I looked around the cafeteria. Nobody was talking much about the locker thief anymore. Earlier that morning, even the teachers who were supposed to be watching us between classes started standing together at the same end of the hall and chatting with each other.

"Have you noticed," I asked Davey, after he was through talking to Tim, "that no one seems too worried about the thief anymore?"

Davey nodded. "I think the locker thief will steal again soon because it looks like the coast is clear."

Out of the corner of my eye, I noticed Mrs. Kieffer walk into the cafeteria. She headed straight for Mr. Newport, who was lunch monitor, and started to tell him something. Her face was all flushed. I could see Mr. Newport's face change when he heard what she said. The two of them hurried out of the cafeteria.

"I wonder what that was all about," I said.

A minute later, the bell rang.

"That's weird. The bell is ten minutes early," Joey Lightfoot said, looking at his watch.

Everyone started to talk at once. Some people stood up and started clearing off their lunch trays. Other kids just sat where they were.

"Maybe there's a loose fuse!" someone yelled.

A few seconds after that, Mr. Gray, the principal, made an announcement over the PA system.

"All fifth- and sixth-graders, please go immediately to your homeroom classes. I repeat. Do not go to your first afternoon class. Please go directly to your homerooms."

I looked at Davey. "Something is definitely up."

As soon as we were all assembled in Mrs. Kieffer's room, she came in and told us to get some work to do, then follow her in a line back to the cafeteria.

"What's happening?" Eben Friedrich asked. He had a bewildered look on his face.

"Mr. Gray will explain," Mrs. Kieffer said. She looked very serious.

We walked back through the halls to the cafeteria. Everyone from the other homerooms were doing the same thing.

When we got there, several tables were already filled up. Mr. Gray was talking in low tones to Ms. Larsen and Ms. Cook.

"May I please have quiet?" he suddenly boomed. He looked around. Instantly, it was silent.

"I am very sorry to report that there has been another theft here at MLK," he began.

Everyone started to whisper and look around. Mr. Gray waited till it was quiet again.

"While any act of theft is a serious matter, this particular theft is especially objectionable to the faculty." He paused. All of us were sitting on the edge of our seats, wondering what he would say next.

"Sometime late this morning, someone came into Mrs. Kieffer's room and stole her grade book out of her desk. Until that grade book is found, the entire fifth and sixth grades will have detention here in the cafeteria."

A buzz went through the crowd.

"At this moment, we are conducting a search of every single locker," Mr. Gray finished. "If anyone can shed light on this incident in the meantime, please come forward at once. Otherwise, I want absolute quiet."

I opened my math book but couldn't concentrate. I was thinking about telling Mr. Gray about our investigation and my hunch about Reed Litwin. Then I remembered what Davey and Nancy had said. Reed may have behaved suspiciously, but so far we had no proof that she was the thief. I would just have to wait until the teachers finished the locker search.

We sat there for a whole half hour. No one except Mary Ann Hockney even asked to go to the bathroom. I noticed that Nancy didn't follow her, and I couldn't say I blamed her.

# OUR SECRET GANG

Suddenly the door to the cafeteria flew open. Mrs. Kieffer came striding through and headed right toward our table. There was a determined expression on her face, as if she meant business.

I glanced immediately at Reed. Now she would get what she deserved—in front of the entire fifth and sixth grades.

Mrs. Kieffer finally stopped at the head of our table and stood there staring down at all of us. *Here it comes, Reed Litwin*, I thought.

But it wasn't Reed she wanted after all.

"Jeanine Hoffman, please come to Mr. Gray's office at once," Mrs. Kieffer demanded.

# 7

· · · · · · · · · · · · · · · · · · · · · · · · · ·

# Accused

I could feel my face turn beet red.

"Me?" I asked. "Are you sure Mr. Gray meant me?"

"I'm positive," Mrs. Kieffer snapped. "Get your things and come."

A bunch of kids had started to murmur. A few even snickered. I noticed that one of them was Reed.

"That will be enough," Mrs. Kieffer told them. They instantly shut up.

Davey gave me an alarmed look, but I couldn't say anything to him. All I could do was gather my things and stand up. I knew I was innocent, and some kind of mistake had been made, but with everybody staring at me, I felt like the thief.

Numbly, I followed Mrs. Kieffer to Mr. Gray's office. Suddenly it dawned on me that maybe this didn't have anything to do with Mrs. Kieffer's missing grade book at all. Maybe it had to do with Ella.

"Mrs. Kieffer, this doesn't have anything to do with Ella Fairfax, our housekeeper, does it? She's been sick lately and . . ."

"No, this has nothing to do with Mrs. Fairfax," Mrs. Kieffer replied.

I couldn't believe how mean she was being. I'm not exactly the class pet, but I'm a good student. I get along with Mrs. Kieffer really well.

Inside Mr. Gray's office, he told me to sit down. Mrs. Kieffer sat down, too.

"I must admit, Jeanine," began Mr. Gray, "I am very surprised that a student of your caliber would do a thing like this. You're just about the last person I would expect to have in here."

"Do a thing like what?" I asked.

"Please, don't try to deny it," Mrs. Kieffer said. "It will only make things worse."

"Deny what?" I asked. "I don't know what you're talking about."

"Jeanine, the missing grade book was found in your locker," Mr. Gray replied.

"In *my* locker?"

"Yes. Unless you've traded lockers with another student, which is against school rules, the grade book was found in your locker, number three-thirty-seven," he replied.

"But I didn't steal it!" I cried. I could feel tears coming to my eyes. I looked back and forth from Mr. Gray to Mrs. Kieffer. "I didn't," I repeated. "You've got to believe me. Somebody must have put it there. Someone wanted to make it look as if I took it, but I didn't."

"You mean to tell me that you think someone planted it there?" Mr. Gray said.

"Yes," I answered.

"But who?" Mrs. Kieffer asked. I could tell she didn't believe me.

"How about the same person who's been stealing from the lockers all week?" I offered.

"You mean to tell me that you think the locker thief is trying to throw us off the trail by making it look as if you're the culprit?" Mr. Gray asked. "That's pretty sophisticated thinking."

"But the locker thief is pretty sophisticated," I replied.

"What makes you think so?" Mrs. Kieffer asked.

"My friends and I in the Millerton Detective Gang have been investigating." Suddenly everything hit me all at once, and I started to cry.

Mr. Gray handed me a tissue. "Here, use this," he said. "Take some deep breaths, then try to explain."

I blew my nose a few times and waited till I felt a little calmer. Then I took a few deep breaths and began. "First, it's hard to steal from the lockers, because even though there are no locks, there are usually people around. And the locker thief must plan the thefts, because Jonathan Turner didn't tell anyone except Ramsey that there was money in his social studies book. The locker thief must have overheard their conversation that morning and come back for it."

Mr. Gray and Mrs. Kieffer looked at each other.

"My friends and I have some suspects. We're about to solve the case. I just know it," I continued.

"Jeanine, I know that you and your friends have solved mysteries in the past," Mr. Gray said. "And someone may have planted that grade book in your locker. But you've got to understand my position. As the head of this school and the person responsible for discipline, I can't simply let this event go. I can't have other students know that the grade book was found in your locker and I simply let you off because you're a good student."

"I'm not asking to be let off. Just let me and my friends try to solve the mystery," I said.

Mr. Gray sighed, and Mrs. Kieffer looked troubled.

Finally the principal cleared his throat. "Normally, in a case like this, I would be forced to suspend you outright from school for a week. I am taking a special exception in this case, however, because of your record and past performance here at MLK."

I sat on the edge of my seat as he continued.

"I'm going to let you pursue the investigation. There are two conditions, however, and you aren't going to like one of them."

"I'll do anything," I promised.

"First, the investigation must be pursued honestly, and your detective gang must break no rules in order to try and identify the thief."

"That's no problem," I said quickly.

"The next condition is, until you have successfully completed your investigation, I am suspending you from basketball."

I looked down. Being suspended from basketball meant I would lose any chance to become captain. And I had wanted to be captain of the girls' basketball team at MLK for as long as I could remember. But it was the only way I could prove that I was innocent.

"Okay," I agreed softly. "I don't really have a choice."

As I got up to leave, I looked at Mr. Gray. "I know that you usually call up the kid's home in cases like this. But Ella Fairfax, the person who takes care of me and my sister, is sick. The doctor thinks she has a bad heart. She's going into the hospital tomorrow, and I'm afraid if she found out about this, it might . . . make things worse."

"I won't call today then," Mr. Gray said. "But you know I'll have to tell your family about this eventually."

"I think the gang and I only need a few days to solve the case," I replied.

Mr. Gray nodded. "I'm going to tell anyone who asks that the grade book has been found under mysterious circumstances. Obviously, the basketball players will know that you've been suspended from practice, but there's not much we can do about that."

"And Jeanine," he added. "Please get in touch with me by the end of the week, so we can discuss what's happened with your investigation."

"Yes, sir," I replied.

I just hoped I'd have something to tell him by then.

By this time, it was last period. I headed to Mr. Newport's classroom for math. Since I was already late, I decided it wouldn't hurt if I was a little later. I quickly wrote notes to Davey, Nancy, and Jason, calling an emergency meeting of Our Secret Gang after school. Then I went and put the notes in their lockers.

When I finally showed up at Mr. Newport's, a bunch of people looked up. But Mr. Newport was writing on the board, so he didn't notice me.

"Jeanine, what happened?" Jenny Roper whispered when I sat down.

I shrugged. "I can't really talk about it yet."

I tried concentrating, but math isn't my favorite subject. Class seemed like it took forty hours instead of forty minutes. I kept on thinking about the awful thing that someone had done to me. Why was I being framed?

Finally the bell rang. I practically ran out of Mr. Newport's room. Still, a few people asked me what happened. I told them the same thing I'd told Jenny. I couldn't talk about it yet.

Davey was waiting for me by my locker when I arrived. "I got your note. What happened?"

"They found the grade book in my locker," I said in a low tone, opening my locker to get my things.

Davey looked shocked. "You're kidding."

"I wish I were," I replied. I looked inside my locker. Nothing seemed out of place or missing.

"You're not kidding it's an emergency," Davey said. "Boy, this is serious."

I nodded.

"What did Mr. Gray say?" Davey asked.

"He suspended me from basketball and gave me till the end of the week to solve the mystery," I replied. I slammed my locker shut.

"Am I glad to find you," Nancy said as she joined us. "There's a nasty rumor going around that you stole Mrs. Kieffer's grade book."

"Who told you that?" I asked.

"Everyone was talking about it. I said that was crazy."

"Someone planted the grade book in Jeanine's locker. The teachers discovered it during the search," Davey said.

Nancy stood there for a second, not saying anything.

"Who would do a thing like that?" she finally whispered.

We decided to walk to Davey's, and on the way, I told the gang everything that Mr. Gray and Mrs. Kieffer had said.

There was a note on Davey's kitchen table from Matta saying that she'd taken Davey's little sister, Annie, to the dentist. I was just as happy not to have to explain everything again. We made some hot cocoa and took it upstairs.

"Let's go over the facts again," Davey began once we were all seated. "Last Monday, a bracelet is stolen from Linda Loomis's gym locker. Meanwhile, Jeanine finds Reed Litwin in the locker room during practice. That fact may or may not be related to the crime," Davey said.

"Thursday, Esther's new red sweater is stolen during fourth period," continued Nancy. "A number of people saw Esther put the sweater into her locker just before art. Reed and five other people sign out to the bathroom during that period. Any of them could have stolen the sweater."

"Friday, Jonathan has twelve dollars taken from his social studies book, which, if you ask me, he stupidly left in his locker," Jason said.

"Just the facts, Jason." Nancy grinned.

"Right. That theft took place any time between first and third periods," Jason went on. "Three of the same names show up on the bathroom sign-out sheets: Reed, Mary Ann Hockney, and Billy Gagliardi."

"We all follow the suspects, but nothing happens Monday," I said. "Tuesday morning, Mrs. Kieffer's grade book is stolen. By the end of lunch, it's already been planted in my locker."

"The question is, Why yours? Why not mine?" Davey asked. "Why not somebody else's?"

"I've thought about that. Somebody either has it in for me or just stuck it in the nearest locker when the coast was clear," I replied.

"Who would have it in for you?" Nancy said. "Everybody likes you. You were even nominated for captain of the basketball team."

"Reed Litwin," I answered. "She's the only person I can think of. She hates me, and the feeling is mutual."

"Also, she's one of our prime suspects," Jason said.

"I've been following her all week. I just can't catch her doing anything," I complained.

Nancy was chewing on her pencil. "I don't

know what else we can do to try and catch the thief."

"Let's look at what's been stolen," Davey said. "Maybe there's some pattern we're not seeing."

"Everything seems to go down in value," Jason pointed out. "First a turquoise-and-silver bracelet was taken, then a new sweater, then twelve dollars, and finally a teacher's grade book."

"Yeah." I said. "The grade book doesn't really fit with the other things. It's not worth anything."

"Unless you want a locker search," Davey said. "Then the grade book was the perfect thing to steal. It got everyone's attention, and it helped create a primary suspect."

"We've got to catch the thief," Nancy announced. "We can't let someone frame Jeanine."

"How about bait?" Jason suggested.

"Bait?" everybody asked.

"Yes. We could plant something valuable in one of our lockers and spread the word we brought it to school. Then if it's stolen, we can ask Mr. Gray to do another locker search," Jason said.

"I've got a new portable radio," Nancy said. "It's one of the yellow ones that you can use for sports. How about that?"

"Nancy, that's too valuable," I protested.

"I've had it since last spring, and I hardly ever use it," Nancy replied. "Besides, if we catch the thief, I'll get it back."

We looked at each other.

"It's worth a try," Davey said.

"I think you're right," I agreed.

Jason nodded.

"Good. We'll start tomorrow," Nancy said. "I'll wear the radio on the bus so everybody notices and leave it in my locker all morning. I can check it after every period."

"Before you leave it in your locker, we can talk about it in the hall," Davey said.

"In the meantime, we'll keep watching the suspects," Jason offered. "Now that the attention is on Jeanine, the thief might steal again."

"We especially have to watch Reed," I added.

"Don't worry, Jeanine," Jason said. "We'll catch this crook."

"I hope so." I sighed.

Davey suggested we all go into town to Mr. Barrie's Sweet Shoppe for banana splits to cheer us up. I didn't really feel like it, but everybody else did, so I went along. And it did make me feel better. By the time we got back, Matta was there so she could drive us home.

# OUR SECRET GANG

When Ella asked about my day, I was careful not to say anything about what had happened. It wasn't too hard. I think she was as nervous about going into the hospital the next day as I was for her. She was a lot quieter than normal.

She seemed most concerned about my missing basketball practice in order to drive her to the hospital. I told her not to worry.

# 8

## New Bait

**B**y the next morning, word had gotten around school that the grade book had shown up in my locker. Some people, such as Cynthia Malinowski and the other snobs who clung to their new celebrity friend, Reed, avoided me entirely. Others, such as Joey Lightfoot, seemed a little embarrassed and pretended to be doing something else when I walked by. A few people came up and said they thought the whole thing was done on purpose, and that someone had it in for me. Jolene Nichols and Ellen Hayes came up and said they were voting for me for team captain anyway.

"Nobody on the team thinks you did it except for Samantha Redburn and a couple of other people," Jolene added, trying to make me feel better.

"Jolene," Ellen said, elbowing her in the ribs.

"Well, it's true," Jolene replied defensively.

"Thanks, you guys," I said. "I appreciate your telling me."

I headed off to my locker. I had put my coat on the hook inside and was taking out my geography workbook for first period before I saw the note. At first, I thought it was from one of the gang, but when I opened it up, I knew I was wrong. The note had been written on a computer and it said:

Dear Jeanine,
I know that you and the Millerton Detective Gang are looking for the person who stole Mrs. Kieffer's grade book. I think that you should look in the least obvious place.

Best of luck.
Signed,
*Anonymous*
P.S. I know you did not take it.

After I'd read the note once, I read it again. *Who could it be from? What did it mean?* I wondered.

I wanted to tell the rest of the gang right away, but the bell for homeroom rang. Then I spotted Davey coming down the hall.

"Hi, Jeanine," he said when he saw me. "Everything with Nancy went great."

"Terrific," I answered. "Wait till you see this." I handed him the note.

"Where'd you get this?" he asked, after he'd read it.

"I found it in my locker this morning," I told him.

"But what does it mean? 'Look in the least obvious place'?" Davey exclaimed. "I wonder who sent it."

"Davey, Jeanine, please take your seats," Mrs. Kieffer called from the door of the classroom. "Everyone else already is seated."

For the rest of the morning, I divided my time between trying to figure out what the note meant and thinking about Ella. I was really worried about her. The closer it got to two-thirty, when Lisette was coming to pick me up, the worse I felt. By lunchtime, I didn't even feel like eating.

"Jeanine, over here," Davey yelled. He and Nancy were sitting together at the far end of the cafeteria. Jason had music this period on Wednesdays.

"Any luck, Nancy?" I asked, sitting down.

She shook her head. "Nothing so far, but we've got the rest of lunch and all afternoon."

She sounded the way I felt—down.

"Show Nancy the note," Davey said.

I pulled it out of my pocket and pushed it across the table. Nancy opened it and read it.

"Wow!" she exclaimed. "This is really something. I wonder who sent it."

"I've been wondering if it's from the thief," I said. "I read once that some criminals *want* to be caught."

"Or it could be from someone who knows something we don't," Davey suggested. "What do you think the advice means: 'Look in the least obvious place'?"

"The least obvious suspect is Mrs. Kieffer herself," Nancy mused.

"That's true," Davey replied, "but Mrs. Kieffer can't be the thief. Who else is the least obvious?"

"I still say Reed did it," I muttered as I played with my tunafish sandwich.

"Speak of the devil," Nancy said.

I looked up. Reed was standing at the end of our table, smiling at me in a strange way. Suzy Fredette and Melinda Dalton stood just behind her, giggling.

"Well, if it isn't Miss Millerton herself," Reed said in a loud voice. A bunch of people nearby stopped talking.

"They might take your crown away now that your reputation isn't so pure. Miss Millerton is supposed to be *honest*," Reed said.

"I am honest," I replied. "And I'm not Miss Millerton."

"Honest? Except in small matters like a teacher's grade book that showed up in your locker," Reed continued. "I suppose you're going to try and tell us someone else did it."

"We've got our suspects," I replied hotly.

"Like who?" Reed asked, rolling her eyes.

By now, she had a whole crowd watching. And by now, I had had enough.

"Like you, Reed Litwin. Nothing started disappearing from people's lockers until you showed up at MLK. And explain how your name is on the bathroom sign-out sheets for every single period in which something was taken. Explain that," I practically shouted.

A couple of people gasped.

"I don't know what you're talking about," Reed said haughtily. But I could tell I had upset her.

"Check for yourself," I continued. "Anybody can check. You signed out during fourth period last Thursday, when Esther's sweater was stolen, and second period on Friday, just about the time Jonathan's money was taken.

"And who was hanging up her sign about the dumb cheerleading squad in the girls' locker room on the day that Linda's bracelet was stolen? I just happened to come in to fix a broken shoelace. You weren't very happy when I came in by surprise, were you? Before that, you'd had the locker room all to yourself!"

"You're just getting desperate for someone to blame it on," Reed said uneasily.

"Or maybe you are!" I exclaimed.

At that, Reed scoffed, and then she marched off. Melinda and Suzy scuttled behind her like a pair of crabs.

I knew I had won the fight. I could tell by the way people acted. Everybody started buzzing as soon as Reed was gone. A few people even tried to tell me they knew I wasn't guilty. But I didn't feel like sitting in the cafeteria anymore.

"I'll see you guys later," I said to Davey and Nancy, getting up. "I've got something to do."

This wasn't exactly the truth, but it wasn't a lie, either. I went straight to the girls' room in the basement, the one nobody ever uses, and cried till the end of lunch period.

# OUR SECRET GANG

*  *  *

Lisette arrived at two-thirty on the dot. I was waiting for her outside, at the top of the school steps. Neither of us said very much on the way home, aside from discussing how furious we were at our parents for not calling back.

Ella was waiting for us in the kitchen with her winter coat on. When I saw the small suitcase that she had packed for staying overnight, I got a terrible lump in my throat. She'd never spent a night away from us before. On the way to the hospital, Ella explained the procedure the doctors would be doing. "It's called an angiogram. I'm on first thing in the morning. Eight A.M. It only takes a little over an hour. I wouldn't normally have to stay in overnight, but they have to monitor my heartbeat and my blood pressure. I should be ready to leave tomorrow by the time school lets out." She almost sounded cheerful, but I knew it was for our sake.

"You'll be okay. I just know you will," Lisette said. But she sounded as if she needed convincing.

"Joseph will heat dinner for you tonight and make breakfast in the morning," Ella informed us. I hadn't even thought that far ahead.

I still hadn't told Ella about what had happened at school. I decided to wait until she was back home tomorrow night.

Once we got to St. Luke's Hospital, everything happened fast. Ella had to fill out a bunch of forms. She asked if she could write Lisette and me in as next of kin instead of her cousin Mavis in Ohio. I think she was trying to make us feel better. A nurse came and took her blood pressure and her temperature. Then another nurse brought us to her room.

"I'm afraid it's time for visitors to leave," the nurse said gently to the two of us.

"Right," Lisette said. She was being more mature than I'd ever seen her act in her life.

"We'll call to say good night," I promised.

"You do that. We won't be able to talk in the morning," Ella said.

Then she hugged us both hard.

"See you tomorrow after school," I said.

"You two behave yourselves, and don't give Joseph any trouble," Ella said.

Then the nurse shooed us out the door.

"Think she's going to be okay?" Lisette asked.

"I hope so," I replied, "but I'm trying not to think too much about it."

# 9

· · · · · · · · · · · · · · · · · · · · · · · ·

# The Thief Gets Caught

**W**hen we got in the front door, the phone was ringing.

"I'll get it," Lisette yelled. "Hello," she said breathlessly into the phone.

"Oh, hi, Mom!" Lisette said. "Hi, Daddy. What? No, I wasn't shouting, I just came in from outside."

"I'll pick it up in the library," I whispered. I went in and picked up the phone just in time to catch my parents giving Lisette a hard time about shouting into the phone.

"I'm sorry," she said in a low voice.

"Hi, Mom. Hi, Dad," I interrupted.

"Oh, Jeanine, hello," my mom said.

"How are you, sweetheart?" asked my dad.

"Well, I could be better," I replied. "You've heard about Ella?"

"Yes," my father answered. "She called us the other day, and we spoke to Doctor Weber just a few hours ago. I know you're a worrier, Jeanine, but he says these tests are just routine. Ella will be fine."

"Well, that's not the way the woman from his office sounded," I replied.

"Now, darling, just listen to your father," my mother said. "Doctor Weber is the best, absolutely the best. If he says it's not serious, it's not serious."

"How's everything else?" my father asked.

"Fine," I answered flatly. I could tell it was going to be another typical call with my parents. In a minute, they would start telling us about what a great time they were having and all the neat people they were meeting.

"I've got some news," my mother said. "Just try and guess!"

"Now, dear, you said you'd keep it quiet," my father said.

"Are you coming home soon for Christmas?" Lisette asked hopefully.

"No, no, it's nothing like that," my mother answered. "Try again."

# OUR SECRET GANG

I was not in the mood to play one of my mother's games.

"I give up," I announced.

"Your father's started playing polo!" my mother exclaimed.

"Polo?" Lisette and I chimed together.

"Well, it's quite the thing here in Palm Beach," my father said. "And my friend Dickie Braganza said—"

"Darling, it's getting late," my mother suddenly interrupted. "The Robinsons' cocktail party starts in half an hour."

"Oh, right. Well, girls," my father said, "that's the signal. We'd better be going. I'll have to tell you about my polo exploits some other time."

"When are you coming home?" I asked.

"Well, we're not exactly sure yet," my mother said, "but we'll know in a few days. We'll call as soon as we know."

"Right, and in the meantime, you two girls take care of our Ella," my father said cheerily.

"Don't worry," I replied.

"Toodle-oo," my mother said. "Remember that Daddy and I love you both very much."

"Right," my father said. "So long, children. We'll call in a few days, when we know about the holidays."

"Bye," I said.

Before Lisette could add her good-bye, my parents had hung up. I went back into the hall to get my book bag.

"I wish they didn't call at all," Lisette said, staring at the wall.

My parents have always favored Lisette, but for the first time, I realized that she found it as hard as I did having them for parents.

That night, after we talked to Ella, I called Nancy.

"Davey, Jason, and I had a meeting while you were at the hospital," she said. "We didn't have any new ideas about who wrote the note."

"I can't figure it out, either," I said. "Whoever wrote it must have some idea of who the culprit is."

"If it had been handwritten, we might have been able to figure out the writer's identity. All Davey could tell was that the note was printed on a dot-matrix printer. And apparently they're very common. The school has six of them in the computer lab."

"Wait a minute!" I said. "I just had an idea. Maybe the writer used a computer at school. Which means that the note would be on one of the disks in the lab. All we'd have to do is figure out who used the disk."

Nancy sounded doubtful. "I guess it's worth a try. We'd have to go through a lot of disks."

"Let's try it," I said. "By the way, did anything happen with your radio?"

"Nope, but we're going to try again tomorrow," Nancy answered.

"Can you meet me at school a half hour early?" I asked. "We'll start going through the disks."

"Sure. I'll call Jason if you'll call Davey," Nancy answered.

When I hung up, I felt a little better. At least we had a lead to follow, and the investigation would keep my mind off Ella.

The next morning, Davey, Nancy, and I met at the computer lab at a quarter to eight. Jason couldn't come because he had to practice French horn, or his mother would kill him.

The door to the lab was open and the lights were on, but Mrs. Minifer, the computer lab librarian, wasn't in yet. A few computer geeks were already in there working, but they barely looked up at me. I'd brought the note with me. The first thing we did was make sure it had come from a printer in the lab.

We checked out all the printers. They were all made by the same manufacturer, and the type matched the print on the note.

"The note probably was printed out here," Davey said. "Good thinking, Jeanine."

"The note had to be written after lunch on Tuesday," Nancy said, "since that's when the grade book was found. Let's see who used the computer room on Tuesday after school or early Wednesday morning."

"Right," I said.

We went over to the log book.

Nine people had signed in between last period on Tuesday and first period on Wednesday.

"It's got to be one of them," Nancy said.

"Let's each take three names and start going through their disks," Davey suggested.

"Isn't that against the rules?" I asked. "I promised Mr. Gray that we wouldn't do anything illegal or dishonest to catch the locker thief."

"Let's ask," Davey said. He went over to

Michael Howells, who was bent over a computer game and talked to him for a few minutes.

"Michael says kids borrow each other's programs and files all the time," Davey reported.

"Actually, I'm supposed to be using a remedial math program," Nancy added. "It might be on one of the disks we look at."

"Okay," I said. "Let's get to work. We don't have a lot of time."

We split up the names. I got Susan Korman, Tim Kennedy, and Oliver Orton. I went and got Susan's disk first, and started to go through her files. It seemed to take forever. Eight o'clock came and went, and I didn't think of Ella once. I was only halfway through Susan's disk when the first bell rang.

"Find anything?" I asked the others.

"Nothing here," Nancy said.

"Or here. It's slow work," Davey said.

Nancy looked at her watch. "We'd better go if we want to plant the portable radio in my locker again."

Davey nodded. "We can come back after school."

"I'll see you at lunchtime," I told them. "I don't want to be around when you do it. It might look suspicious."

# Shannon Gilligan

I stayed in the computer lab a little longer, going through Susan's files, but I didn't find a thing. I decided to come back and try Tim Kennedy's disk during my study hall, last period today.

The morning passed more quickly than I thought it would. I kept an eye on Reed. I thought about Ella, who was done with her test by now. According to the rest of the gang, whom I talked to between classes, there were no suspicious moves by any of the prime suspects. By lunch, no one had touched Nancy's radio, either.

My first period that afternoon was music. Ms. Anderson is the music teacher. She's new this year, and she's really different. We used to sing hymns and partriotic songs all the time. Now that's all changed. On Halloween, Ms. Anderson made a tape recording of scary sounds, so we got to groan and shriek all we wanted. Today she walked into the classroom carrying two bongo drums and a burlap sack filled with rattles made out of gourds.

"Class, we're going to listen to a recording of African percussion music today. Then we're going to try and play it ourselves," Ms. Anderson announced.

A bunch of kids cheered. Eben Friedrich let out a whoop and started playing the bongo drums the minute Ms. Anderson passed them out.

# OUR SECRET GANG

About ten minutes into the record, a siren went off. It wasn't an ambulance kind of siren. It sounded more like a police car. At first, I thought it was background on the record. Then I realized it was coming from outside our classroom.

"What on earth is that?" Ms. Anderson asked, heading toward the door.

Just as she opened the door, somebody shot out of Mr. McClure's door across the hall.

"It's Tim Kennedy!" Evie Woods cried. "Where's he going?"

Everyone ran to the door to see what was going on. A bunch of kids spilled into the hallway. The door to one of the lockers up the hall was open and the siren sound was coming from inside.

"Look! It's Tim's locker! It's rigged with a siren!" someone yelled, pointing.

I'm pretty tall, so I could see Tim Kennedy standing near his locker. He had a firm grasp on Linda Loomis's arm.

"She did it!" Tim yelled. "She stole Mrs. Kieffer's grade book. She stole everything! She's the locker thief!"

Linda's face was beet red, and she was looking down. No one said a word. We were all too shocked. Finally Mrs. Kieffer walked forward.

"Is what Tim's saying true, Linda?" she asked.

Linda didn't say a word. She just stood there, staring at the floor.

"I think you'd better come with me," Mrs. Kieffer said. She took Linda by the shoulder and headed in the direction of the principal's office.

As soon as they had disappeared around the corner, everybody started talking at once.

*Linda Loomis?* I thought. *Quiet Linda Loomis, who seemed so shy, and was now a shoo-in for team captain? What about her bracelet? Had she just pretended it was stolen?*

All of a sudden, it hit me. Of course—Linda's bracelet *hadn't ever been stolen.* She'd just said it was. That was what the note writer meant by, "Look in the least obvious place." We'd never suspected Linda, because she was one of the victims.

"Boy, you and your friends are really good at solving mysteries, Jeanine," Eben said to me, back inside the classroom.

"Yeah, but we didn't solve this one," I replied.

"What do you mean? I thought Tim rigged his locker with that siren to catch Linda," Eben said.

"I think he did, but he's not in the Millerton Detective Gang."

# OUR SECRET GANG

I suddenly remembered that Tim's computer disk was the next one I was going to go through during study hall that afternoon. I bet that he was the person who wrote the anonymous note. He had to be! But how had he known then that Linda was the thief?

Ms. Anderson tried going back to the African drums, but it wasn't much use. Everyone was too excited. She finally gave up and let us all talk while she played the bongos herself up in the front of the room.

Everybody in my class wanted to talk to me at once.

"Linda obviously did it because she was jealous," Jenny Roper announced. "She wanted to be team captain and make sure you didn't have a chance."

"Getting me suspended from basketball certainly helped her chances," I agreed.

"Practice hasn't been the same without you," Ellen said. "Are you going to come this afternoon?"

"I can't," I replied. "I have to go pick up somebody in the hospital. But I'll be there tomorrow."

"Who's in the hospital?" Ellen asked.

"Ella Fairfax, the woman who takes care of me and Lisette," I answered. "She's got heart trouble."

"Boy, you've had a rough week," Ellen said.

"I know," I answered. "But I think my luck just changed."

While we were talking about Linda, I noticed Tim Kennedy walk by in the hallway with Mrs. Kieffer. She must have gone to get him. They were headed up to the front office. About twenty minutes later, just as music period was ending, Tim knocked at the classroom door.

"Mr. Gray would like to see Jeanine Hoffman," he told Ms. Anderson.

"You tell him, Jeanine!" Eben Friedrich yelled.

"Go for it!" a couple of other kids shouted.

I followed Tim into the hall. He was heading back to his class.

"Wait," I whispered. We were alone in the hall for just a few seconds. "I want to ask you a question."

Tim stopped and looked at me.

"You sent me the anonymous note, didn't you?" I asked.

Tim looked at the floor and turned red. Then he glanced back at me and nodded. With that, he turned around and dashed into Mr. McClure's room.

*So, it was Tim Kennedy! Wait until I tell the gang*, I thought.

When I got to the principal's office, Mrs. Kieffer and Mr. Gray were waiting for me.

"Jeanine, sit down, please," Mr. Gray began. He cleared his throat nervously. Out the window, I saw Linda getting into a car. She was with her mother, who looked pretty angry.

"The first thing I want to do is apologize for everything that's happened this week," Mr. Gray began. "We did the best we could with the information we had."

"But you've been punished unfairly," Mrs. Kieffer broke in. "Linda Loomis just confessed to all the thefts that have occurred recently, including the theft of my grade book."

I nodded. "Why did she do it?"

They exchanged a glance.

"We would have brought you down here sooner, but we had to notify Linda's parents first," Mr. Gray continued.

"You're a mature girl for your age, Jeanine, and what we're about to tell you is strictly confidential,"

Mrs. Kieffer said. "However, we feel that it's your right to know this."

"Mrs. Loomis wasn't too surprised when we called her this afternoon with our news," Mr. Gray said. "Apparently, Linda has stolen before."

I waited for him to continue.

"According to Mrs. Loomis, Linda stole something from her about two years ago. It appears that both Linda's parents have busy careers, and they think she was trying to get attention. As you know, Linda is very shy, and an only child besides. Stealing might be the only way she knows to make herself the center of things."

"Why did she put the grade book in *my* locker?" I asked.

"She wanted to be team captain very badly," Mrs. Kieffer explained. "The surest way to do that was to put you out of the running."

"But what if you'd believed my story about the grade book's being planted?" I asked. "Then I would still be in the running for captain, and Linda wouldn't have accomplished anything."

"Even if Mr. Gray hadn't suspended you from practice," Mrs. Kieffer said, "Linda assumed that people would have gossiped about you. That would probably have done enough damage."

"You still *are* in the running for team captain," Mr. Gray said. "I've suspended Linda for the next five days. I believe that the vote for captain is tomorrow. Is that right?"

I nodded, thinking about everything I'd just heard. In a way, I felt sorry for Linda, even though what she'd done had caused me a lot of trouble. She must have really felt desperate.

I stood up.

"Before you go," Mrs. Kieffer said, "tell me how you rigged up the siren in Tim's locker."

"Uh, that wasn't our idea," I replied.

"So Tim Kennedy solved this case on his own?" Mr. Gray asked, surprised. "He made it sound as if he'd just been helping you out."

I nodded. "He found the locker thief."

"Well, good luck with the election tomorrow," Mr. Gray said.

"And thank you for coming down, Jeanine," Mrs. Kieffer said. "I'm so glad everything has worked out."

"Me, too!" I replied.

# 10

## Great Minds Think Alike

I was dying to talk to the gang, but Lisette was picking me up at two-thirty to get Ella. I left everybody a note saying we *had* to talk soon.

When we pulled up to the front of the hospital, Ella was waiting with her bags outside near the curb. She must have been eager to get out of there, I thought.

"Ella!" I yelled as soon as the car stopped and I could jump out.

"Hi there, sweet pea." She gave me a huge hug. "Hello, Miss Lisette," she added, kissing my sister, too.

"Well?" I asked. "How was everything?"

She gave us a big smile.

"My heart's fine," Ella began. "The angiogram

went very well. But my cholesterol count is out of sight. We've got to change our diets, girls."

"That's all? You just have to watch your cholesterol?" I asked.

"That, and I need to take some megavitamins," Ella replied. "But it's nothing serious."

"I'm so glad," Lisette said.

"Me, too, Ella. I thought you were going to die," I said.

Ella laughed. "Well, I'm not, not if I have anything to say about it. Now, let's get out of here. The nurses were nice, but this hospital is driving me crazy."

On the way home, we discussed what the doctor had said and how Ella would have to start cooking differently. It sounded as though we were going to be eating a lot more the way Davey's family did— all sprouts and soybeans and stuff.

"But enough of all that. What's new with you?" Ella asked.

"You're not going to believe it," I said.

"Try me," Ella replied.

So I did, starting with the missing bracelet and leading up to the stolen grade book, my suspension from basketball, and Linda's admitting everything.

"My poor baby," Ella moaned. "And you didn't say a word!"

"I didn't want you to worry," I said. "Besides, I knew we would find the culprit."

"But you say that this Tim Kennedy was the one who solved the case?" Ella asked.

I nodded.

"Well, I'm going to call his mother when we get back and thank her," Ella announced.

"You can't. He doesn't have a mother," I replied. I didn't know this for sure. I'd never asked Tim, and he was new this fall. But Jason had told me that his mom had died last year from cancer.

"Then he probably needs a good meal. Why don't you have him over for dinner?" Ella said. "I have to thank him somehow."

"Okay, but I have to get to know him first," I said.

"That's what you said about Reed," Lisette reminded me, but she was smiling.

When we got home, I called Davey. First I gave him the great news about Ella. Then I told him that Tim Kennedy had written the note.

"How did he know it was Linda?" Davey asked. "That's what I want to know. I didn't have a clue."

"None of us did. I'd like to invite him to our meeting on Saturday morning to find out how he solved the case," I said.

"Great idea. I'll call him tonight and ask him," Davey said.

As soon as we hung up, I called Nancy and Jason to tell them about Ella and Tim Kennedy.

The next day, there was a note from Davey in my locker.

Dear Jeanine,
Jason and Nancy can't make it tomorrow, so the meeting is changed to dinner tonight at my house. Maybe after this afternoon, we'll have something besides solving another mystery to celebrate. (Hint, hint.)
Tim will be there.

*OSG*
*Davey*

The celebration he was talking about was for my getting elected team captain. I didn't know what would happen now that Linda was out of the race, but I did know I was nervous about going back to practice.

I saw Reed in the hallways a couple of times

between classes. Even if she was a jerk, I wanted to apologize for accusing her of being the locker thief. But she kept on avoiding me. Finally, right before lunch, I saw her standing by her locker. Suzy and Melinda were there, too, but I decided to go ahead, anyway.

I took a deep breath.

"Reed, I want to apologize for the things I said the other day about your being the thief," I began.

Reed whirled around and looked at me hotly.

"I was wrong," I continued, "and I shouldn't have accused you. Please accept my apology."

Reed stared at me for a few seconds. "I'll think about it," she finally snapped, before turning around and marching off. Melinda and Suzy were so shocked, they just stood there with their mouths open. Reed was so nasty, even her friends were speechless.

I just shrugged and headed to my locker. No matter what I said, there was no way we could ever be friends. I'd made my apology, and there was nothing else I could do.

Practice finally rolled around. Coach Kimball gathered us all on the court and started to make a short speech to welcome me back and explain about Linda. Before he could finish, Jenny Roper interrupted him.

"Coach Kimball," she yelled, waving her hand. "Coach Kimball!"

"Yes, Jenny, what is it?" he asked curtly.

"Sorry to interrupt," she said. "But a bunch of us were talking at lunch, and we thought that considering what's happened, we'd like to elect Jeanine our team captain unanimously. Besides, this will save time, and we can get right to work. Our first game is Tuesday," she added, as if anyone needed reminding.

"Yes, Jenny, thank you," Coach Kimball said. He looked around at the rest of the squad. "Who would like to go along with Jenny's proposal?" he asked.

People started raising their hands, but I was too nervous to look. The next thing I heard was Coach Kimball saying, "Okay, then, it's unanimous. Jeanine Hoffman is the new captain of the MLK girls' basketball team, soon to be number one in the district."

With this, he blew his whistle, and everyone started cheering and clapping. I don't know if it was for me, or for becoming first in the district, but I felt great.

"Hello, Jeanine," Matta said cheerily that night as I arrived at Davey's. She was pulling some bread from the oven. She always bakes on Fridays. "I heard that you've had quite a week."

"Yup. You can say that again," I said.

"Well, I'm delighted to hear Ella is fine. I could have told her she had high cholesterol without her having to go to the hospital," Matta announced. "You're going to have to change your diets, eat more the way we do."

"Yes. Ella told us," I replied, smiling.

"Tell me, did you get elected team captain?"

I nodded.

Matta came up and gave me a big kiss, saying, "That's my girl. Good for you. Now hurry on up. I think everybody's there."

I ran up the back stairs and burst into the attic. Davey, Nancy, and Jason were all there, and so was Tim Kennedy. Davey had a liter of cola waiting and five glasses.

"Did you win?" he asked.

"Unanimously," I replied.

"Hooray!" everybody yelled.

"I knew it!" Nancy said. "I knew you'd win."

Davey started pouring soda into the glasses. "Here, everybody, take one. Let's make a toast to Jeanine."

"Here, here," everybody else said. We all raised our glasses and then sipped our colas.

"Tell Jeanine what you told us about the mystery, Tim," said Nancy.

"I was just about to ask," I said.

"It was all luck at the beginning," Tim began. "I saw Linda Loomis at the store last Saturday, and I noticed that she was wearing the bracelet that she had said was stolen. Or if it wasn't the same bracelet, I thought it was strange that she would have another one just like it.

"At first, I thought she had found it. But then, on Monday, I heard her complaining to somebody on the bus about losing the bracelet. That's when I started getting suspicious," Tim continued.

"When did you become certain?" I asked.

"I didn't really, but I kept an eye on Linda, and there were a couple of things I noticed," he replied.

"Wait till you hear this, Jeanine," Jason said.

"I noticed that Linda looked over at you a lot. If I saw her in the cafeteria or something, you always seemed to be nearby, and she would be staring at you. I couldn't figure out why. I didn't know she was running against you for basketball captain."

"You mean she was following me?" I asked.

Tim nodded. "At least it looked that way. When the grade book showed up in your locker, I put two and two together."

"But what about the siren in your locker?" I asked.

"Well, I suspected that Linda had done the other thefts, too, but I wasn't certain. So I decided to write her a note and tell her that I knew she was the locker thief. I said that there would be something in my locker that might be of interest to her, especially if she wanted me to keep quiet about it," Tim said. "I didn't sign the note. I just gave her my locker number."

"And then you rigged your locker with a siren, so that when she opened the door, you could catch her red-handed," I said.

"Right," Tim replied.

"How did you do that, anyway? The siren, I mean?" I asked.

Tim gave me a long, complicated explanation of how he had rigged up the siren by using wire and an old car stereo speaker and a bunch of other stuff. I didn't understand a word of it. But I remembered that day at lunch when he had been discussing electronics with Davey. He sounded as if he knew lots about it.

"Well, I have just one other question," I told Tim when he was finished.

"Shoot," he said.

"When you wrote me the note, why didn't you sign it?"

Tim turned beet red. "Well, I knew that the Millerton Detective Gang liked to work alone, so I didn't want to barge in." He looked at his watch. "I'd better get going now. My dad's expecting me."

"Wait. You're supposed to stay for dinner," Davey said. "Matta is making homemade pizza. She's counting on you."

"Really?" Tim asked shyly.

"Really," I said.

"Stay, Tim. We're going to watch a video after dinner," Nancy added.

"My mom can drive you home," Jason chimed in.

"Okay. I'll go call my dad," Tim said.

Davey told him where to find the phone. The minute Tim was gone, Davey and I both started to speak at once.

"You go," he said.

"No, you first," I replied.

"Well, I don't know what the rest of you think, but I've got a suggestion," Davey began.

"Let's ask Tim to join the gang," Nancy interrupted.

"Wait! That was *my* idea!" I said.

"No, it wasn't. I thought of it first," Davey said.

"You were going to suggest the same thing?" I asked.

"Great minds think alike," Davey remarked.

"It's decided then," Nancy said. "I mean, as long as Jason agrees."

So far, Jason hadn't said anything. We all looked at him.

"I definitely think we should ask Tim to join. I like him a lot, and he knows a lot about electronics and computers. We can use someone like that. But I want to get one thing straight—" Jason paused. There was a devilish grin on his face. "It was *my* idea to invite him in," Jason said.

"Jason!" I exclaimed, "You're too much!"

• • • • • • • • • • • • • • • • • • • • • • • • • • • •

*Now that you've learned Jeanine's secret, you'll want to learn the other gang members' secrets, too! Find out new member Tim Kennedy's secret in the next book about Our Secret Gang,* Science-Lab Sabotage. *In that book, Tim also helps the gang find out who's been trying to ruin a top-secret science experiment.*

*Here's a scene from*
**Science-Lab Sabotage:**

When Leonard and I got to dog obedience class, Mrs. Peckham was just starting. She was right in the middle of a speech about how licking the face of a human was "intolerable" when Leonard jerked his head up and pricked up his ears.

"What is it, Len?" I asked.

Suddenly he started to bark. He was straining at his leash and looking toward the hallway.

"Maybe he has to go to the bathroom," I said to Mrs. Peckham. "I'll be right back."

I went out to the front lobby and unhooked Leonard's leash near the front door. But instead of going outside, he ran in the opposite direction.

"Leonard!" I yelled. "Leonard, stop! Where are you going?"

Mrs. Peckham came out into the hall.

"What's all the commotion, Tim?" she asked.

"I don't know," I answered. "Leonard just ran away. I'll go get him."

I took off after Len, but he was nowhere in sight. The hallway was dimly lit, and I could barely see in front of me. After I made a few turns off the main corridor, I thought I was in a part of the junior high that I'd never seen before. But then I recognized something—the smell. We were in the science wing.

Ahead of me I heard Leonard let out a few growls and then a high-pitched bark.

"Len?" I called. It was eerily quiet.

Suddenly I heard a chair squeaking across the floor of one of the classrooms. There were some other noises, too, which I couldn't make out. I opened the door to the nearest classroom and peered into the half-dark room. It was the biology lab. Inside a tall figure was bent over, with his back to me.

• • • • • • • • • • • • • • • • • • • • • • • • • • • • •

## Our Secret Gang's
## GUIDE TO USING SECRET CODES

*You will not always have the time or materials to write an important secret message in invisible ink. For those times, you can use a secret code. There are lots of good secret codes to use. What's important is that everybody in your detective agency knows which code you're using and agrees to it. Discuss it first and choose one that everybody likes.*

The simplest code is to spell everything backward. Try and decipher the codes below:

1. pleh dnes

2. emoh tnew ew

3. truh neeb s'yevad

Good work! Another way to use the same code, but make it harder, is to eliminate spaces between the words. Try to figure out these samples:

**4.** tididdeer

**5.** rekcolymmorfgnissimsioidara

**6.** eerhttasigniteemeht

Another, completely different code uses the third letter in every word of a nonsense sentence to spell a word. All the sentences together spell a message. Try and see if you can figure out the messages below.

**7.** Anchor soon Emma Lee. Train attack. Slow hunt sacks cleaning.

**8.** Magazine feelers hat. Anthill aches teenyboppers. Happy slow selling slicks nice scenes.

See the key to messages below. Good luck detecting!

**Key to secret codes:**

*Words spelled backward.*

1. Send help
2. We went home
3. Davey's been hurt

*Message spelled backward without spaces.*

4. Reed did it
5. A radio is missing from my locker
6. The meeting is at three

*The third letter of each word forms a message. Each sentence equals one word.*

7. Come at once
8. Get the police

# About the Author

Shannon Gilligan graduated from Williams College in 1981. She has written numerous children's books, including several books in the Choose Your Own Adventure series. Her Choose Your Own Adventure book *The Case of the Silk King* was recently adapted as an hour-long special for NBC Television.

Ms. Gilligan likes to ski, fish, play squash, and read. She spends two or three months a year traveling. The rest of her time she spends at her home in Warren, Vermont, with her husband who is also a writer.

She is currently at work on several creative projects.

## Are you a good detective?
## Solve tricky mysteries with
## ENCYCLOPEDIA BROWN!
# by Donald Sobol

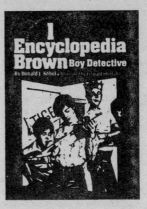

Match wits with the great sleuth in sneakers Leroy (Encyclopedia) Brown! Each Encyclopedia Brown book contains ten baffling cases for you to solve. You'll find mysteries such as "The Case of the Worm Pills" and "The Case of the Masked Robber."

Get ready for fun with the great detective! You'll want to solve each one of these mysteries. Order today!

# Magical Skylark  Adventures!